A Tapestry of Poems

A Tapestry of Poems

Marietta Pereira

Bigfoot Publications
Because, there's a writer in everyone.

A Tapestry of Poems
Author : Marietta Pereira

First Published by
Bigfoot06 Publications (OPC) Pvt. Ltd.
1st floor, BSR Building near Vishal Mega Mart,
Daultabad Flyover, Laxman Vihar Phase 3,
Gurugram, Haryana (122001)
Website: www.bigfootpublications.in
Email: info@bigfootpublications.in

First Edition : November, 2023

ISBN Print Book - **978-81-19512-54-6**

Typeset in Baskerville Old Face 12pt
by Yachika Prajapati For Bigfoot06 Publications

Printed in India

CONTENTS

A Schoolbag of Memories

Four decades have winged by;
Since I crossed a T and dotted an I
Within the portals of Sacred Heart High.

Looking back with so much nostalgia
I sift through my memorabilia
And through the past I let my mind wander...

Standing in line for morning assembly at 9
Drill, athletics, mathematics
That sometimes caused dreadful colic.

Rotation and Revolution
Fractions and chemical reactions
Not everyone's cup of tea.
Yes, I remember ol' Allauddin Khiliji!

March Past eliminations and examinations
At the time, matters of great consternation!
Elocution and debates always on our plates.

Sports Day, Hip-hip Hurray!
Who's going to carry the cup away?
Kho-Kho, Kabbadi
Weren't they the favourites of everybody!

Singing ditties was so much fun.
Like those lunches, we shared beneath the sun...

Teachers strict, yet always kind
The ones who helped us get thro' the grind –
"Love Conquers All", they reiterated
Lifetime values they inculcated.

The self-control bell
Meant you just couldn't yell
And a two-minute impatient silence fell.

There was happiness and sadness
And more than an ounce of madness
In that very dear school
Where we had to live by the rules.

Night

When the light of day softly fades away,
When that flaming ball of fire is all set to retire,
When children hasten home after play,
When Raven and Sparrow fly home yonder,
When bright city lights dispel the darkness of the night,
When the star-spangled skies are a delight to the eyes,
When moonbeams cast a silvery sheen.

When work is done and the day's race is run
When we whisper a little prayer-
Thank you, dear God, for your love and care.
Your blessings we seek every day, everywhere!

So What Would My Diary Say To Me?

My diary
From a corner in the closet
All sad and teary, would say to me
Where have you been?
We haven't met lately.

At twenty, you wrote aplenty
I knew your secret crushes
And what brought on your blushes
I knew what made you happy
And what made you mad or sad.

You poured out your heart to me
Your dreams and aspirations
Your longings and frustrations
When ma yelled
And Dad waited for you to come home.

What's this I see you engrossed in?
Twitter, Facebook, Instagram
This virtual world
I simply don't understand
My head is spinning, my heart is breaking
Could you spare a thought for me?
Tell me you still love me.

Dear Mirror

I think you don't quite see it all
Silvered and salted hair I'd fain conceal
But my tender heart
By deeds, I shall reveal.

Zeroing in on that extra inch or curve
On the surface can't you discern that steely nerve?
You dwell upon line and wrinkle
But don't you see the merry eyes that twinkle?

Never mind that double-chin
There is a gentlewoman hidden deep within
My jeans alas have gone three sizes larger
I don't think I can stretch them any farther.

Mirror, dear mirror,
My sagging figure and face
I know too well have sadly fallen from grace
But underneath that drab and flab, you see
Is a beautiful, warm and spirited me.

A daughter, a wife, a sister or a mother
To my parents, husband, children or brother
I bring to all I do the feminine touch
If not for me, their lives would lose so much.

One day at a time is all to which I aspire
In your esteem may I rise just a little higher?

Memory Lane

Walking down memory lane,
My heart wrenches in nostalgic pain,
At the thought, it'll never, ever happen again.
My mind's eye sees flashes of
Faces and places long gone by...

Of classrooms and teachers;
Ribbons and tiffin;
Long, lazy summers and cosy, cuddled-up winters;
Fairy tale books and furtive looks;
Junk food and pickles;
Crushes and puppy love.

Of gully cricket;
Of being bitten by the chicken-pox bug;
Lectures bunked and subjects, well,
- almost flunked

Of college picnics and movie tickets;
Of church choirs and sitting around the fire.
The voices, the choices, the favourite haunts
With friends, I hung out with -

Once so near,
Now draw a wistful smile and
A bitter-sweet tear...

US

There are a zillion people on the planet
There is you and me,
There is he and she,
There are they and them,
And there is a 'We' and an 'US',
That sets the buzz.

It is the US that stands strong,
It is the US that makes right every wrong,
Together WE shall find the strength,
Together WE shall tackle every bend,
In the US there is magic
Isn't that Fantastic?
Let US walk hand in hand
Bringing peace, justice and happiness to every land.

The Honey Called Money

A piece of paper with a number
That may bring you happiness
Or turn your life asunder.

It is so precious
You cannot afford to be reckless
You don't want to miss that gorgeous necklace.

Earn, save and then spend
Must absolutely be your trend
You might not be helped by a friend.

Help someone in need
Do not succumb to greed
Let that be your creed.

Childhood

Happy smiles, playful ways
Innocence and giggles
Marked our childhood days.

What joy a birthday brought!
As did writing that letter to Santa
With great thought.

Homework was a chore
Yikes! A horrible bore.
Chocolate cake and candy bars
We devoured with unabashed glee.

Shed a tear when we bruised a knee
Bedtime tales, rhyme and verse
Yes, childhood was also made up of these.

A life so simple
Caste and creed did not matter
Just happiness...no anger.

Lock

Lock envy and greed
Don't go by colour or creed.
Lock malice
Be generous, not callous
Seek to stall injustice.
Lock fear and anxiety
Practice piety.
Make your dreams come true
Lock hurdles that deter
Lock the negatives
It's being positive that takes you through.

Tears

Sadness brings them on
So does gladness
Don't hold them in
Let them out
You will feel better
Without a doubt.

The bogeyman

He's a bogeyman
He's loved and adored
By the mathematician and the nerd.

Not me.
I shiver and quiver
At the mention of his name
He's also caused me
To hang my head in shame.

Mother tells me to make friends with him
But that is just so terrible a thing
I'm never able to figure him out.

Numbers, equations and problems
Give me a headache
That no pill can take away.

I wish I could be rid of him
Run away to a land
Where he does not exist
Then how happy I'd be
Living life bogeyman-free.

Success

It's more than 9 to 5
It's your will and wish
It's a couple of risks
It's your persistent push.

The Tree

Once upon a time
There was a tree
Deeply rooted in the earth
Its branches spread wide
Thriving in the sunlight.

It provided shade and shelter to man and beast
It was home to chirping birds and scampering squirrels
Its green leaves gently danced in the breeze.

Then shorn of its beauty and grace
It longed to be upright again
And feel the freshness of the rain.

No birds, no nests,
No little children
Climbing up in zest.

Beloved tree!
You were in pain
Felled were you for trade and gain.

Fight

When you fight
To show your muscles and might
It could turn into an awful sight
Fight for what you think is right.

Escalator Anxiety

I say an escalator is as fearful as a creepy-crawly alligator
A moving staircase
That would be straight out of a Harry Potter.

My friends join me in the elevator
Cajoling me to step on the scary people - mover
I am terrified!
Ha Ha! An escalator to me only spells disaster.

The Sunflower

Walking through a field of gold
It is the sunflower that I behold
A golden-green delight
She stretches out to the sun so bright.

This stately beauty
Has so much to give
Oil and seeds
To help us live.

Your winning ways
Make my day
You are a dear, sunflower
So pretty, positive, generous and gay!

On Children's Day

They have stayed awake late
After having too much plum cake
Spotty skin, runny nose
They sure do keep you on your toes.

They've been scribbling on the walls
Interrupted your telephone calls
Often driving you nuts
With their 'ifs' and 'buts.'

And yet,
You are there to banish their blues
And kiss away their boo - hoo - hoos.

You beam with pride
At hesitant steps or furious stride
One so shy, another so bold
Each little treasure
Is yours to have and to hold.

No malice and hatred
To drive you wild
No guile, no violence
Only sweet, sweet innocence.

Thank you, Lord
For the joys and the tears
Let us keep them close through the coming years.

Missing You Ma

Your quiet demeanour
Your patience and understanding
We shall always remember.

You bore with fortitude
The storms of life
Until Jesus opened heaven's door.

Quietly a light went out
Darkness came about
But in heaven, the angels sang aloud:
"Ma's come home."

Heartbroken as we are
We know you're happy, you're safe
Free from pain
Free from worldly stress and strain.

A treasure trove of sweet memories
You've left behind
Ma, we love you, miss you ma.

Rain

Blue skies turn to grey
Loud claps of thunder
The heavens open
Blobs of silver
Filling every river and bay.

How green is the grass
How inviting the petrichor
The parched earth
Fresh and alive
Truly, how refreshing!

On Disappointments

It is okay to be down in the dumps
When you experience life's many bumps
Don't fret for too long
Tomorrow is another day
A new beginning is on its way.

On Your Birthday Dear Motherland.

May you be clean and green
May your children learn and play; and not be exploited in any way.
May women trod freely the paths they choose
Without the obstacle of gender - specifications and sexual abuse

May you be devoid of scams and monetary jams
May the old and lonely find love and care
May caste, creed and race not have an ugly face
May humanity thrive in every place.

May good be appreciated and evil defeated
May progress happen and setbacks lessen.
Jai Hind!

Learning From The Master

Jesus told us parables aplenty
Teaching truths
So that we may bear good fruit.

The mustard seed, so small
Slowly grows wide and tall
God's kingdom is like the mustard seed
That grows to embrace one and all.

Jesus calls us to be the yeast
Raising the dough
Making people love Jesus more.

The parable of the sower
Helps us realise
That neither rocky ground nor thistles must we be
But good soil that produces a crop, a hundredfold, sixty or thirty.

The good seed and the weed
Exist side by side
On Judgement Day God will decide.

If the treasure we are to obtain
Let us detach from material gain
On the last day
The Master will separate the good fish from the algae.

The Lamb of God

Jesus was born in a manger
To the Virgin Mary and Joseph, a carpenter:
He shed His precious blood,
That we might be redeemed,
And to our Heavenly Father surrender.

Teaching through parables, working miracles,
Changing hearts while angering the Pharisees!
Faith, said He, could move mountains...
Forgiveness of utmost importance...
Good triumphs over evil, always.

Then betrayed by Judas...by Peter denied,
Condemned to die, scourged and crucified...
From the dead, He arose
To give new life and hope
To man through the ages, worldwide.

Flowers

Fragrant blooms of varied hue
The good Lord created just for me and you.

In pots and gardens
In bouquets and garlands
In grief and in joy
In hello and goodbye.

In homes, churches and temples
Or simply growing wild
Flowers are one of a kind.

Dreams

When dreams are born
Don't let them die
Chase them like a lion chasing its prey.

The chase might be long and hard
Clouds and rain mar your path.
Don't give up
Until you make them come true
And then you'll wake up a happier you.

Hope

She quietly creeps in
While you wallow in despair
You rush to greet her
You cajole her to stay
She calls herself 'hope'
She helps you cope.

What My Cell Doth Say

You knew my ancestors
Then you get acquainted with me.
I brought to you
A whole new world
To experience and see.

You text and forward
Call and search
Click selfies so many
Post a greeting or a prayer
Spicy gossip you do share.

I wake you up each morning
Lest you sleep all day.
You shop and pay your bills
Even order your pills
I guess I'm quite indispensable.

To your children
I'm a big distraction
You tear your hair in frustration.
When I ring
I'm often out of reach
Then we play a game of hide and seek.

When I'm lost
You're so forlorn
I wish I could wipe your tears
As you think
I'm forever gone.

You've been advised
Not to look at me
Soon after you awake.

And switch me off
An hour before
You bid the day goodbye.

It's hard, I know
To adhere to advice so severe
But use me well
And your life will be swell.

Against All Odds

Life's hardly a bed of Roses
I must tackle a curve ball every day

Amid fear and hopelessness
Despair and frustration
Against all odds
I must stand straight and tall
I've got to keep the faith
Believe that it is not the end of it all.

Never mind if situations resolve at their own pace
I'll simply carry on with God's abiding grace.

Corona

A virus so nasty
Having effects so ghastly
Sickness and sadness
Gloom and doom
Enveloped our planet
Morn, night and noon.

But we soldiered on
Fighting to eradicate
This virus that left us
At hell's gate.

Freedom

Oh to be free!
Just to be me
To say as I please
To stay or to leave.

To hold on, to say no
To learn and discern
To marry or to live alone.

It's my life
I choose to live it
As I please.

Story Behind My Name

Mother looked everywhere
And was quite filled with despair
She couldn't find a name
For her little baby bear.

Then in a book that she had been reading
She chanced upon one, long and rare
Marietta would she call me
And that's who I am
To mom, dad and aunty Pam.

Without The Letter B

You wouldn't see the bright yellow sun,
Nor would there be any butter and a bun.

No pretty butterfly would fly by
You wouldn't have a balloon to hold up high.

You wouldn't hear a bell ring
You wouldn't hear the birds sing.

Nobody would have a brain
You wouldn't have a bicycle to ride down the lane.

How would you be ‘blessed', ‘brilliant’ and the 'best'?
If 'B' didn't fit in with the rest.

Waiting For a Letter

Excitement and anticipation
Until the letter arrives
Watching the clock
Racing to the letterbox
Peering inside
Has the letter arrived?

Disappointment
Will tomorrow be my lucky day?
I can't say.

315 Poem

Don't be afraid
Pray
Help is on its way.

My 333 Weekend Poem

Two golden days
When I unwind
Gone too soon.

My 333 Commitment Poem

Night and day
I love you
In every way.

©YourQuote.in

Unrequited Love

He is in her dreams
There is longing in her heart
He doesn't care
His heart is elsewhere.

F Letter Poem

Friends and family
Fill our lives with
Fun and warmth.

543 poem

The aged need your love
They cared for you
Be their sunshine!

My 333 Departure Story

Carrying with me
Your love bug
In my heart.

Dear Father,

It has been 29 long years since you left
Strong, brave and full of jest
You ably took care of our little nest.

You were loving and kind
Helping us the right path to find
Prayer was important to you
Hence values and ethics we knew.

Always a song on your lips
I fondly remember riding on your scooter
Enjoying the many trips.

Dad you were a gem.
We know it now, we knew it then.

My Reverse Poem

Don't get yourself into a dither
Know that life can be sweet, sour or bitter
Just go with the tide
God is always on your side.

My ATM Poem

After we parted
There was a lesson to learn
Marry in haste, repent at leisure.
@YourQuote.in

My 3-Line Love Poem

Walking through the woods
Hand in hand
Planning a future.
@YourQuote.in

Bookmark

You love to read
But the day is fraught
With tasks and chores
That is a complete bore.

You place me on the page you leave
Fancy, quirky or just plain
You use me again and again.
@YourQuote.in

The Friends I Made When I Was Young

The friends I made when young
Stand beside me through thick and thin
They are my source of comfort and strength.

We laugh and reminiscence
Of times long gone since
The good old days were such fun.

Now living life as destined
Walking different paths
There's still that beautiful invisible bond
That never allows us
To be far apart.

@YourQuote.in

Writing to end each line with G.

I woke up to the sweetest birdsong
I smiled the whole day long
Nature sure helps me get along.
@YourQuote.in

The Difficulty of Being Good

There's temptation and distraction
There's greed and desire
There's 'just this once.'
Oh dear! I can't be good all the time.

There's procrastination, sloth and envy
Pride vies with humility
Being good is a difficulty.

I try to be the best I can
Stand up to what I think is wrong
But I may falter
I am human, not divine.

@YourQuote.in